RETURN TO RAVENS PASS

EYES IN THE SKY

by Ailynn Collins

illustrated by Amerigo Pinelli

STONE ARCH BOOKS
a capstone imprint

Published by Stone Arch Books, an imprint of Capstone
1710 Roe Crest Drive, North Mankato, Minnesota 56003
capstonepub.com

Library of Congress Cataloging-in-Publication Data is available
on the Library of Congress website.

ISBN: 9781666346107 (hardcover)
ISBN: 9781666346114 (paperback)
ISBN: 9781666346138 (ebook PDF)

Summary: Ethan keeps having the same nightmare. A huge creature
stares out from the night sky. But then, the dream changes and the thing
points to a row of houses. Ethan is sure something sinister is stirring in
Ravens Pass, and he's determined to find out what.

Image Credits:
Shutterstock: blushfish_ds

Designed by Hilary Wacholz

TABLE OF CONTENTS

You tried to get away, but you couldn't help returning to this odd little town. Every time you wandered, you stumbled onto its streets. It sits along the highway, and off the beaten path. It's in the depths of a forest, and in the middle of a desert. It's surrounded by mountains, and balanced on the edge of a deadly cliff. It's the place where weird things happen, where the unreal becomes real.

Welcome back to **RAVENS PASS**. It's been waiting for you.

CHAPTER 1

NIGHTMARES

Ethan could feel the dream beginning. It was the same dream he'd had all week.

It started with a feeling of being watched. Suddenly, he was standing at his window, looking out at the starry night sky. Then *they* appeared.

Eyes. There were eyes in the sky.

The first time Ethan had had the dream, he woke up screaming and rushed to his parents' room. Afterward, he'd felt ashamed. What twelve-year-old still ran to their parents after a nightmare?

When Mom had led Ethan back to his room, the sky was just the sky. And when she had asked what the dream was about, he was too embarrassed to say.

But this was now the sixth night in a row he'd had the nightmare. Ethan was sick of being terrified every night and tired every day. So, at breakfast the next morning, he decided to get his family's help. He told his parents and big sister, Sabine, about the nightmare.

"The dreams are so real," Ethan finished. "How do I make them stop?"

"I say you should stop reading those scary sci-fi books of yours," Mom said.

"Especially right before bedtime," Dad added.

"Maybe your brain is helping you make up a new story," Sabine said. She twirled a lock of pink hair in her pixie cut. "Maybe you just need to finish the dream and find out how the story ends."

A chill ran through Ethan. "I don't know. This is nothing like the stories I usually write." He thought for a moment. "Do you think my brain is trying to send me a message instead?"

Sabine shrugged. "How would I know? It's your brain." She pushed away from the table and picked up her car keys. "But if you want a ride to school today, you'd better get over it and hurry up."

That whole day at school, Ethan felt haunted by the nightmare eyes. He kept glancing at the windows, half expecting to see them peering back. He could barely focus on his classes. He had to do something.

That night, Ethan went to bed determined to stare back at the eyes. It didn't matter how terrifying the idea was. He lay under the covers till he finally felt the familiar sensation of being watched. Then he found himself at the window.

There they were! Two eyes. Each one was about the size of a full moon. They were dark and shiny with streaks of red. They floated in the sky, staring right at him.

Ethan blinked several times. *When did I even fall asleep?* he wondered. It spooked him how real this dream felt.

"What are you trying to say, brain?" he whispered to himself.

Maybe because Ethan had asked that question, something new happened. To the right of the huge eyes, a grayish blob appeared. Ethan thought it was a cloud at first. But then the blob grew larger. It grew larger and larger until he realized—it was a fingertip. And the giant, knotted finger was coming for him.

CHAPTER 2

A CLUE

The knotted finger stretched out, but then it turned away from Ethan's window. Instead, it pointed to the left.

Ethan was frozen with terror. But soon his curiosity grew bigger than his fear. He leaned to see what the finger was pointing at.

Rows of yellow-roofed houses appeared floating in the sky. They hovered above Ethan's neighborhood. The finger touched a house in the middle of the third row. It tapped the roof.

"W-what's so special about that house?" Ethan asked quietly.

The eyes widened for one long breath. Then the finger pointed right at Ethan. In the next moment, the finger and eyes and yellow houses disappeared into the darkness. The night sky was empty again.

Ethan's heart was thumping hard, but he was excited. *I did it!* he realized. *I faced my nightmare. But . . . what does it mean?*

He had grown up in Ravens Pass, and he didn't know of any neighborhoods with yellow-roofed houses. But the finger had pointed to a yellow roof, and then to him. There had to be a connection. He felt a certainty deep inside his chest.

As Ethan climbed back into bed, he knew what his next step had to be. He would need to find the yellow-roofed houses.

On his walk to the school bus stop the next morning, Ethan searched the street for yellow roofs. He was pretty sure he wouldn't find any, but stranger things had happened in Ravens Pass.

He paused on the sidewalk in front of an empty house. One of the strange things had happened there. His best friend, Avi, used to live at the house. They had been friends since kindergarten. Then suddenly at the beginning of sixth grade, Avi was gone. His family's house was cleared out. No explanation. Just gone. What was worse, no one else seemed to care. It was as if Avi and his family had never existed.

VRROOM!

A loud rumble jolted Ethan out of his thoughts.

"Oh no!" Ethan cried as the yellow school bus drove away down the street.

He sighed. He would have to take the public bus. He walked the extra half mile to the stop. As he arrived, a bus headed into downtown Ravens Pass, the opposite direction from school, pulled up.

Ethan's mind started to race. He couldn't solve the mystery of his friend's disappearance. But maybe he could solve the mystery of his nightmares.

He stepped onto the bus.

I'm going to find the yellow-roofed houses, he thought as he sat down. *Even if I have to ride all through town. And even if it means getting in trouble for skipping school.*

The bus rumbled on. Ethan kept his eyes peeled as they passed city hall, the library, and the office building where his mom worked. No yellow roofs.

Then the bus turned a corner. It headed to the very edge of town. Ethan had never seen this part of Ravens Pass before. His parents had always said there was nothing out here but farmland.

Ethan pressed his face against the bus window. The rolling hills were dotted with trees. Cows grazed lazily in green fields. The bus tilted upward as it climbed a hill. When it crested over to the other side, Ethan gasped.

In the distance was a community of houses, all lined up in neat rows. Every house had a yellow roof!

CHAPTER 3

AN OLD FRIEND

Ethan hopped off the bus at the next stop. The eyes in the sky had definitely led him to this housing development. He only had to find out why.

As he walked down the street, Ethan couldn't help but notice how quiet the neighborhood was. Even if most people were at work or school, there should still have been some activity. The occasional car or delivery truck going by. Someone mowing a lawn, or jogging, or walking a dog. But these streets were eerily empty.

Ethan went up to a house. The curtains were all drawn. He couldn't see inside.

Should I knock? he wondered. *What would I say? "Hi, I've been having nightmares about your house. Do you have a large, scary creature living here with you?"*

He sighed. No, he would likely get dragged away by the police or something.

Ethan kept walking through the neighborhood of yellow-roofed houses. By the fifth block, he still hadn't seen any signs of life or found a single window he could look through. He was getting tired. He sat down on the curb.

"What am I doing?" he muttered. "This can't be right."

Someone crossed the street in front of him. It was a boy about Ethan's age. The boy walked at a rhythmic pace. His back was completely straight, and his eyes were focused forward.

Ethan knew this boy very well. "Avi?" he called.

The boy turned. It was definitely Ethan's old best friend. He had the same dark brown hair and thick eyebrows. He still wore tortoiseshell framed glasses. When they used to play superheroes at Ethan's house, Avi was always Turtle Man because of those glasses. He had said they gave him super vision.

Avi has been in Ravens Pass all along? Ethan wondered, stunned.

Avi said nothing. He just frowned at Ethan, turned back around, and marched away.

Ethan got up and followed after his friend. He called out again, but Avi kept walking stiffly like a robot. Avi finally stopped in front of a yellow-roofed house. It was the middle one in the third row.

Just like in my dream! Ethan realized. He caught up to his friend and touched his arm.

Avi spun around. "Please leave me alone," he said in an odd, flat tone.

"Avi, it's me," Ethan said, taking a step back. "We're friends! We used to go to Ravens Pass Elementary. You came over to my house every day after school. Don't you remember?"

Avi frowned again. His eyebrows almost touched in the middle of his forehead, creating deep creases. "I have never been to Ravens Pass Elementary. I do not know you. Please go away."

Ethan huffed. "Why don't you recognize me?"

Avi climbed the four steps to his front door. "Leave," he replied. "Or you will regret it."

Avi opened the door just enough to slip through. Then he slammed it shut. The loud *click* of the lock echoed all the way down the street.

CHAPTER 4

THE WALL

Ethan stared at the closed door. He backed away from the house and walked as his head swirled.

Did I do something to make Avi mad? he wondered. *Why was he acting so weird? And did my dream bring me to this creepy neighborhood to find him?*

Ethan stopped and looked around. He thought he had been retracing his steps, but he must have taken a wrong turn. He didn't recognize the park that spread out before him. Across the open field was another development. In one corner, he saw a bus stop.

I need to get home, he decided. *I need time to think.*

He quickly passed by the playground when—

BUMP!

Ethan fell backward onto the ground.

"OW!" he cried, rubbing his forehead. He stared at the space ahead of him. There was nothing there to bump into.

Did I . . . imagine things? he thought. *My forehead sure didn't.*

He got up and took small steps forward. He kept his arms stretched out.

THUD!

His hands came into contact with something hard, yet he saw nothing. He pressed against this invisible wall. It wouldn't budge.

Ethan stared at the houses on the other side of the park. Then he looked back at Avi's neighborhood.

They're the same! he realized. The houses across the park were a reflection. The wall was like a mirror, only not. Because Ethan wasn't in the reflection—just the houses.

He walked right, running one hand over the invisible wall. He came to the edge of the park and kept going, determined to find the wall's end. He walked for at least twenty minutes. Yet he could still feel the barrier.

"None of this makes any sense!" he said.

Ethan pounded his fists against the invisible wall. The hits didn't make a sound.

"What's going on?" he shouted in frustration. "Why is this wall here? Why can't Avi remember me? And what does all this have to do with the eyes in the sky?"

Ethan didn't know who he was yelling to, but maybe someone would answer.

No one did. No one came out of their home. Not a single curtain was pulled aside to peek at what Ethan was doing.

Then suddenly the blue sky above grew dark. Ethan watched as gray clouds rolled in. A gust of wind blew him backward, away from the wall.

"*Go home*," the wind seemed to howl.

Ethan shook his head. Wind couldn't speak. His mind must have been playing tricks on him.

The wind increased and whipped the boy in a circle. Ethan grew dizzier by the second. Round and round he went, until he lost his footing. He could feel himself falling.

And just before his body hit the ground, Ethan blacked out.

CHAPTER 5

PRISONERS

Ethan rubbed his eyes and stretched. The early morning sky outside his bedroom window was just turning a pale blue. One puffy cloud floated slowly across his view.

He sprang out of bed and checked his alarm clock. It was the next morning.

What? Ethan thought. *How did I lose a whole day? I was in that neighborhood, then the wind knocked me down . . . so how did I end up back in bed?*

He had so many questions, his head hurt. Whatever was going on, it was stranger than any story he had ever come up with. He needed help making sense of everything. He slipped out of his room and knocked on his sister's door.

No answer.

Very quietly, he opened the door. Sabine was sitting up in bed, staring out her window.

"Hey," Ethan whispered. "Is everything okay?"

Sabine turned. She didn't yell at him for entering her room uninvited. Instead she said, "I had the strangest dream. There was a monster in the sky and houses with——"

"Yellow roofs?" Ethan finished.

Sabine nodded. "It felt so real."

Ethan let out shaky breath. He sat down beside his big sister and told her everything.

"Something is going on in Ravens Pass," Ethan finished. "Something bad. And I think my nightmares, and yours now, are warnings. They're telling us that we need to do something. Will you help me?"

Sabine stared at Ethan. Then she stood up and said, "Get dressed. We're going out. Now."

Sabine was already waiting for Ethan when he came downstairs. It was so early that Mom and Dad weren't even up yet. Sabine scribbled a note for them. Then, the kids sneaked out of the house.

Ethan wanted to ask what Sabine had planned. But the look on her face was so serious, he didn't dare open his mouth. Soon, they came to the top of the hill overlooking the development. Sabine gasped.

"When were those houses built?" she asked. "Mom and I were here a few months ago, practicing for my driving test. It was just an empty field. How—"

"Park here," Ethan interrupted as she turned into the neighborhood. "We don't want to run into the invisible wall."

"The *what?*" Sabine said.

Ethan led his sister to the park. She rushed ahead. Before Ethan could stop her, she bumped into the barrier.

"So the wall is real?" Ethan just had to check. "It's not my imagination?"

"This is definitely real," Sabine replied. She pressed her hands against the seemingly empty air. "How far does the wall go?"

"I'm not sure. I wasn't able to find the end, so it has to be long. Who knows, it might even surround the whole town," Ethan said.

Sabine bit her lip. "Wouldn't that mean no one in Ravens Pass can leave?"

"Maybe," Ethan said. His heart skipped a beat. "We might all be prisoners and not even know it."

"How is it that no one's—" Sabine began, but Ethan had stopped listening. He was staring at someone walking down the street.

"Avi!" Ethan called. He ran to his friend. Sabine followed behind.

Avi looked at them and frowned, as he had done before. "I'm supposed to do something, but I can't remember . . ."

"Maybe we can help you," Ethan said.

Avi shook his head. "Please go home. You are entering dangerous territory." With those strange words, he walked away.

Sabine and Ethan trailed after him. Like last time, there was no one else about. When Avi entered his yellow-roofed house, Sabine exchanged a look with Ethan.

"We have to keep following him. We need answers," she said.

They climbed the four steps to the door. Ethan's heart pounded as he turned the doorknob and pushed. The door opened.

Ethan and Sabine stepped inside.

CHAPTER 6

NIGHTMARE ON TV

Avi's house was quiet and neat. It smelled like lemony floor cleaner. Ethan was reminded of those model homes that people visited when looking to buy a house. You just knew no one lived in them.

Where did Avi go? Ethan wondered.

Sabine led the way into the kitchen. The counters were shiny and unstained by food or fingerprints. They headed to the family room. It was dimly lit, with the curtains pulled shut. Their footsteps didn't make a sound on the plush carpet as they entered.

Before them sat a family, still as statues.

Avi sat straight up in a chair. On the sofa, Ethan recognized Avi's parents and two sisters. They were also perched on the edge of their seats. It looked as if they were ready to run at a moment's notice. They all stared at the TV on the wall.

"There's nothing on the TV," Ethan whispered. The family didn't even blink at the sound.

"Wait," Sabine said, walking farther into the room. "You can see what they're watching from this angle."

Ethan joined his sister. As he came closer, he saw it.

The TV screen showed an image of outer space. Stars twinkled against a dark background. In one corner was a creature. It was also watching the twinkling stars. Its head was long and oval. And it had dark, bulging, orange-streaked eyes.

Ethan's stomach twisted. "Those eyes look very familiar," he said.

Sabine shivered. "It's the monster from my nightmare."

"And all of mine," Ethan added.

As their voices echoed through the room, the creature on the TV turned its head. It looked right at the siblings.

Ethan blinked. He wanted to run. But between his fear and curiosity, his legs wouldn't budge.

The creature moved forward. Just as its head filled the TV, the screen rippled. A four-fingered hand pushed through and reached into the room.

Ethan couldn't catch his next breath. His eyes were fixed on every detail of the hand as it wriggled closer. Its skin was wrinkled and pale gray. Its joints were swollen. The fingers uncurled and stretched toward Ethan.

Sabine screamed. The sound seemed to wake Avi from his trance. His eyes met Ethan's for a split second.

"Help!" Avi whispered hoarsely.

The hand jerked away from Ethan. It darted toward Avi on the other side of the room.

With the creature distracted, Sabine yanked Ethan by the arm. She dragged him out of the house and slammed the front door shut.

Ethan was panting. "The nightmare creatures are real! And they're messing with Avi and his family! We need to save him!"

"What can we do?" Sabine cried, wrapping her arms around herself.

Ethan looked out at the other yellow-roofed houses. Something clicked in his head. "Avi might not be the only one in trouble," he said. "Let's check on the neighbors. You go that way. I'll try the other side."

With one last glance at his friend's house, Ethan ran to the next home. He knocked. No one answered. When he tried the door, it was unlocked.

"Hello?" he called as he stepped inside. "Is anyone home?"

In the family room, Ethan saw six people. They were sitting in exactly the same position as Avi's family had been.

That's Mom's old boss! Ethan realized. He recognized her and her family from an office party he had attended with his parents last year. *Mom said they had moved suddenly.*

The family was staring at the TV. Ethan didn't try to check the screen again. Instead, he shook the kid nearest to him, but there was no reaction. He tried two more houses. The scenes were exactly the same.

Ethan's legs felt as if they were made of jelly as he ran back to Sabine's car. She was already buckled in.

"I was right," Ethan said. His stomach clenched. "It's not just Avi. We need to help all of them."

Without saying a word, Sabine started the car. She pulled out of the development. When they stopped again, they were parked in front of the Ravens Pass police station.

CHAPTER 7

ENOUGH IS ENOUGH

"I've had enough of this joke," the police officer said, crumpling up the report she had been filing. Ethan and Sabine sat on the other side of the desk. Sabine was still shaking. "There's no development in that area of Ravens Pass. It's a swamp. Nothing can be built on that land."

"But, but, but . . . ," Ethan said.

The police officer sighed. "Go home, kids. I have more important work to do than listening to ridiculous stories."

Back in the car, Ethan and Sabine sat in silence. They stared out at the residents of Ravens Pass going about their daily lives.

"Those creatures must have put everyone under some kind of spell," Ethan said finally. "So that no one notices people disappearing."

"Or the development across town," Sabine added. "Or the invisible wall keeping everyone in."

"And for some reason, we're not affected." Ethan took a deep breath, feeling an urgency rise in his chest. "I don't understand what the creatures want! They seem to have an extra-hypnotic hold on the people in the yellow-roofed houses. But the creatures also appear outside our windows every night, telling us to visit the neighborhood. Why?"

Sabine sighed. "I don't know. But the bigger question is, what now? We can't get help. What else can we do?"

Ethan drummed his fingers on the dashboard. An idea began to form in his head. He looked up at the sky. "It's almost night. That's perfect."

"Why?" Sabine asked.

Ethan slammed his palm down, making Sabine jump. "We're going to confront the creature from our nightmares!"

• • •

That night, Ethan lay in bed and stared at his ceiling. Sabine sat in a chair by the window.

"Are you sure this is a good idea?" she whispered.

"We have to do something," he replied, ignoring his racing heart. "If we don't, we could end up like Avi and his family."

Waiting was difficult. Ethan was exhausted from nights with little sleep. His eyelids grew heavy. Then suddenly Sabine gasped, and Ethan sat up.

There, against the night sky, were the eyes.

Every limb was trembling, but Ethan forced himself to step up to the window. He opened it.

"Hey!" he shouted. He felt Sabine's hand on his arm. It was a silent warning to be careful. "What do you want?"

The eyes focused on Ethan. He held his position, refusing to give in to the rising terror.

"What have you done to Avi?" Ethan shouted. "To all those families?"

The eyes grew larger in the sky as they moved closer. Slowly, an oval head became visible. Something clicked in Ethan's brain. This wasn't the same being he had seen on the TV earlier. These bulging eyes were streaked red, whereas the ones on the TV had been orange.

SCRREEEEEEEEEEEEE!

A high-pitched screech filled the night. Goosebumps rose up all over Ethan's body as he cringed at the sound.

Sabine covered her ears with her hands. "Stop! Leave us alone!" she screamed at the creature.

In a flash, the four-fingered hand reached out and grabbed Sabine. It pulled her from the bedroom.

Ethan scrambled through the window and onto the roof. "Let her go!" he yelled.

The creature ignored him. It stared at the screaming girl in its grip as if she were a most interesting snack. Then the hand started to shrink back into the night.

"No!" Ethan cried.

Without thinking, he leaped off the roof. Everything that happened next seemed to move in slow motion.

Flying through the air, Ethan reached his right hand out for Sabine. It barely brushed her foot. In the next breath, he swung his left hand forward. His fingers closed around his sister's ankle. He now dangled beneath Sabine, holding on tight. He would not lose her.

The hand kept pulling up into the dark sky. The rush of air tugged on Ethan, but he tightened his grip on Sabine. Out of the corner of his eye, he could see his neighborhood growing smaller and smaller. He felt sick.

Then unexpectedly, the hand twitched, and Ethan's fingers slipped. He plunged through the air. The last thing he remembered was his sister screaming his name.

CHAPTER 8

EXTRATERRESTRIAL

Ethan blinked his eyes open, but everything was blurry. He felt sore and was glad to be lying in bed. Except, the bed was hard and cold.

Ethan rubbed his eyes, and his vision cleared. He wasn't in his bedroom. The floor and walls were black and smooth, like a dark mirror. The bed beneath him was a white plank standing on metallic legs. There was no other furniture, no windows. Light came from somewhere overhead, although he couldn't see the ceiling.

But as Ethan hopped off the bed, the thing that struck him most was that there was no smell. The room didn't smell clean or dirty. There was no scent of trees or flowers, like in his bedroom. He breathed in. Nothing.

"Hello? Is anyone there?" he called.

He looked up. Familiar eyes peered through from above.

"Where's my sister?" Ethan demanded. "What have you done with her?"

SCRREEEEEEEEEEEEE!

The creature screeched again. Ethan yelped and covered his ears.

But the sound started to change. It became softer. Then the screeching broke up into shorter sounds. They were like words of a language Ethan didn't know. Until—

". . . you understand?" the creature asked.

"Yes!" Ethan said, amazed. "That's my language."

The creature made a sighing sound. "Now we can communicate."

The being dropped down from above to stand in front of Ethan. Except, it wasn't really standing. It hovered above the floor. Strips of cloth hung from its torso, like multiple tails of a kite. It was at least twice as tall as Ethan.

"Where's my sister?" Ethan asked, less angry this time. He was relieved that this creature had made an effort to be understood. "What do you want with us?"

The creature blinked. Its eyelids moved from the bottom to the top.

"Exhibition," it replied.

"What does that mean?" Ethan asked.

The creature turned to the wall across from Ethan's bed. A panel appeared. The creature touched a button with its knobby finger. The dark wall cleared. What Ethan saw confused and scared him.

On the other side was an enormous hall. Giant glass bubbles floated about in neat rows. They were filled with decorations. More of the nightmare creatures hovered around the bubbles. They seemed very focused on the decorations inside.

Along the walls of the hall were large windows. Ethan saw nothing but stars outside. Except, at the bottom of one window, he spotted a green and blue planet with swirls of white.

"That's . . . Earth, isn't it?" he asked the creature.

"Planet called Earth," it replied.

"Where are we?" Ethan whispered, but he already knew. He was in a spaceship somewhere among the stars.

CHAPTER 9

ALIEN MUSEUM

Ethan pressed his face against the clear wall of his room as the spaceship flew farther away from Earth. He had read many space stories before. He had even written a few. But he never believed that aliens were really *real*. And he never thought he would be kidnapped off his planet.

"I want to go home!" Ethan cried.

"But home here," the alien creature said.

It touched another button.

SHLOOOOP!

The wall melted away completely. The alien drifted into the hall. It stopped by a bubble in the second row. It beckoned.

As Ethan walked over, the giant bubble lowered to his height. The closer he got, the more familiar the decoration inside felt. When he was close enough to touch the bubble, all the breath left his body.

The "decoration" was Ravens Pass. His town had been shrunk and captured inside a bubble that floated in the hall of a spaceship.

Then Ethan realized, *The invisible wall going around Ravens Pass. It was this bubble all along!*

He peered in closer. He saw his school. Kids were playing soccer in the field. His eyes traced the streets from school to home. Mom was getting in her car. Dad was walking toward the bus stop to get to work.

"Hey! Mom! Dad! I'm here!" Ethan yelled, banging his palms against the bubble. He whipped around and glared at the alien. "Where's my sister? What have you done with her?"

The alien pointed back at the bubble. Ethan followed the finger and saw Sabine leaving the house. Her pink hair glinted in the sunlight as she got into her car. She drove off toward the high school.

"Doesn't she notice I'm missing?" Ethan asked. "Doesn't anyone?"

"No notice," the alien said. "You erased from memories."

Ethan's swallowed the lump in his throat. Just as Avi had forgotten about their friendship, the aliens had made Ethan's family forget about him. It would be as if Ethan had never existed.

"Why?" he asked, tears coming to his eyes. "Why would you do all this? Why take my town?"

The alien screeched for a second. "Study. We collect many primitive species," it said. It was as if the alien was learning to speak better with each sentence. "Your town is the only one from planet Earth. Many advanced species enjoy seeing and learning about our collection. We travel from quadrant to quadrant. We spread knowledge."

Ethan's mouth dropped open. He stared out at the other bubbles, the other communities. "This is a traveling zoo? A museum? You've stolen lives, and you're turning us into your intergalactic entertainment!"

CHAPTER 10

FACT IS STRANGER THAN FICTION

"Exhibits don't know they are here," the alien said. "We take good care of them. No harm, no foul—as humans say."

"But I know," Ethan said. He blinked away the tears. "And I am harmed."

A soft screech came behind him. "Yes! Agree!"

Turning around, Ethan saw another alien. Something about it looked familiar.

"It's you! You were the one who came to my room!" Ethan cried. The red streaks in the alien's eyes were a dead giveaway. "You brought me here."

"Yes. You saw me in sky," the red-eyed alien said, nodding. "I wipe your memory, like others. But you don't forget. And more are remembering."

The other alien sighed. "A few humans are resistant to our methods. That is why we have the special neighborhood to keep them out of trouble."

Ethan looked back at the bubble holding Ravens Pass. "The yellow-roofed houses," he realized. "So Avi and all those other people were remembering things, and you just moved them there? It's not right!"

"That is what I tell Chief," red-eyes said. It turned toward the other alien. "Never has an exhibit had so many problems!"

"Please, let my town go," Ethan added. "You can't just play with people's lives like this!"

The alien called Chief focused its bulging eyes on Ethan. "We can find a better way to wipe memories. We will keep you on the ship for study and—"

Before Chief could say more, red-eyes let out a loud screech. More ear-splitting sounds echoed through the hall as Chief replied. Ethan didn't have to understand them to know that they were arguing. Other creatures floated over to listen.

As the arguing continued, hope began to rise in Ethan's chest. Maybe red-eyes was helping him again. Maybe Chief could be convinced.

Suddenly, Ethan had a thought. "You know, in zoos on Earth, some animals have to be put back into the wild," he called out. Both aliens fell silent and focused their bulging eyes on him. "A few years ago, people in Ravens Pass protested the big city aquarium keeping octopi. Octopi are too intelligent. They don't do well in captivity."

"Don't do well?" Chief repeated.

Ethan's heart raced. He had to keep going. "Yes. Maybe it's the same with Ravens Pass. More people are remembering, right? I bet soon I won't be the only one whose memory you can't wipe. What would your customers say if all the humans had to be brought on board for study? Or if you had to move everyone into the yellow-roofed houses to live like zombies? It would be bad for business."

Chief rubbed its chin with a hand, which felt oddly human to Ethan. Red-eyes and the other aliens who had gathered around screeched quietly. Ethan held his breath.

Finally, Chief spoke. "Maybe it is time to release Ravens Pass 'back into the wild,' as you say."

Ethan exhaled. Red-eyes let out a chitter.

"But not you. You have all your memories," Chief added.

"I—I'll never tell," Ethan said in a rush, his hands shaking. He couldn't spend his life on the spaceship. His heart hurt at the thought of never being with his family again. "No one would ever believe me anyway! Alien abductions are the stuff of science fiction. Please let me go home!"

Red-eyes started screeching again. Ethan was sure it was pleading with Chief too. After a minute, the sounds stopped abruptly. Before Ethan could ask what they had decided, Chief stretched out a knotted finger.

The alien touched Ethan on the head, and the boy fell asleep.

• • •

When he woke up, Ethan was back in his room in Ravens Pass. He jumped out of bed and ran down to the kitchen. His family was at breakfast. They were chatting happily as if it was an ordinary Saturday.

Ethan laughed. "Mom, Dad, Sabine! You are all here!"

His family looked at him, baffled. "What are you talking about, Ethan?" Dad asked.

"I was afraid you might be moving to that development on the other side of the hill," he replied.

"There's no development out there, silly," Sabine said. She stuffed another piece of pancake into her mouth. "Have you been having those weird dreams again?"

"Yeah . . . I guess," Ethan replied. "But could you drive me out there anyway, just so I can see the real place? I need to convince my brain."

Sabine arched her eyebrow, but then let out a sigh. "Fine. Let's go."

"Come back soon," Mom said, grinning. "We have a surprise for you."

Sure enough, the development with the yellow roofs was gone. Ethan ran into the empty field and tried to find the invisible wall. It was gone too. He let out another laugh as he got in the car.

When Sabine and Ethan walked back into the kitchen, Avi was helping himself to a pancake.

"Surprise!" Mom said to Ethan. "I thought we could take a trip to the zoo today, and I invited Avi to come along. There's a new exhibit."

The word *exhibit* sent chills through Ethan, but he pushed the feeling aside. He ran to hug his friend instead. "Avi! I've missed you so much!"

Avi held out an arm to stop him. "Whoa, E. We were only away for a week on vacation. Why so dramatic?"

Ethan stepped back to catch his breath. He almost couldn't believe it. Ravens Pass was on Earth again. Everything was truly back to normal.

He laughed and high-fived his puzzled best friend. "Right. I guess it just felt a little longer."

Ethan kept smiling as he grabbed his own breakfast. He knew he would never be able to tell his friend or his family the truth. Like he had promised the aliens, no one would believe him.

But maybe, one day, I'll write the story, he thought. *It'll become a best seller, for sure.*

TALK ABOUT IT

1. Ethan went to his big sister for help. In what ways did Sabine help out her brother? Point to specific examples in the story.

2. Do you think it was a good choice for Ethan to confront the creature in the sky? What would you have done?

3. Were you surprised when aliens were behind Ethan's nightmares and the strange things going on in town? Why or why not?

WRITE ABOUT IT

1. If other beings did come to Earth, what do you think would happen? Write two paragraphs describing it.

2. Ethan often felt scared, but that didn't stop him from acting. Make a list of at least three times when he overcame his fears.

3. What happens next? Does anyone else get their memory back? Are the aliens gone for good, or do they return to Ravens Pass? Write the story.

AUTHOR

Ailynn Collins enjoys creating tales for kids, from wild science fiction to spooky mysteries, and has authored many fiction and nonfiction books. When not writing, she mentors young writers or participates in dog shows and sports with her five dogs. She lives near Seattle.

ILLUSTRATOR

Amerigo Pinelli is an artist from Naples, Italy. He also teaches at the local comics school and runs art workshops for kids. It's a great way to never get bored. Although life with his wife, Giulia, and his three daughters, Chiara, Teresa, and Irene, is already plenty exciting.

GLOSSARY

ABDUCTION (ab-DUK-shun)—the act of taking someone against their will

BECKON (BEK-uhn)—to give a wave, nod, or other motion that tells someone to come

CAPTIVITY (kap-TIH-vih-tee)—the state of being kept in one area, under someone's control

EXHIBIT (ig-ZIH-buht)—a display that shows something to the public

EXTRATERRESTRIAL (ek-struh-tuh-RES-tree-uhl)—a being that comes from outer space

HYPNOTIC (hip-NAH-tik)—able to put people in a sleeplike state where they're not aware of what's happening around them

PRIMITIVE (PRIM-uh-tiv)—relating to an early stage of technology or development

RESISTANT (rih-ZIS-tuhnt)—able to not be affected by something

DISCOVER ALL THE WEIRD TALES OF RAVENS PASS